AUTUMNAL

based on the television series created by
JOSS WHEDON

"The Heart of a Slayer" written by CHRIS BOAL

"The Cemetery of Lost Love" written by TOM FASSBENDER & JIM PASCOE

penciller CLIFF RICHARDS

inker JOE PIMENTEL

colorist GUY MAJOR

letterer CLEM ROBINS

These stories take place during Buffy the Vampire Slayer's fourth season.

TITAN BOOKS

publisher
MIKE RICHARDSON

editor
SCOTT ALLIE
with ADAM GALLARDO and MICHAEL CARRIGLITTO

collection designers
KEITH WOOD and DARCY HOCKETT

art director
MARK COX

special thanks to
DEBBIE OLSHAN at FOX LICENSING,
CAROLINE KALLAS and GEORGE SNYDER at BUFFY THE VAMPIRE SLAYER,

Buffy the Vampire Slayer™. Autumnal. Published by Titan Books, a division of Titan Publishing Group Ltd. 144 Southwark Street London SE1 0UP. Buffy the Vampire Slayer™ & © 2001 Twentieth Century Fox Film Corporation. All rights reserved. TM designates a trademark of Twentieth Century Fox Film Corporation. The stories, institutions, and characters in this publication are fictional. Any resemblance to actual persons, living or dead, events, institutions, or locales, without satiric intent, is purely coincidental. No portion of this book may be reproduced, by any means, without express written permission from the copyright holder. A CIP Catalogue record for this title is available from the British Library

PUBLISHED BY
TITAN BOOKS LTD.
144 SOUTHWARK STREET
LONDON SE1 0UP

FIRST EDITION
NOVEMBER 2001
ISBN: 1-84023-382-6

1 3 5 7 9 10 8 6 4 2

PRINTED IN ITALY

what did you think of this book? we love to hear from our readers.
please email us at: readerfeedback@titanemail.com or write to us at
the above address.

Art by CHRISTIAN ZANIER
with DAVE STEWART

THE HEART OF A SLAYER

YEAH, WE SURE DID GET THOSE DEMONS, BOY. THEY WERE REALLY...GOTTEN.

I MEAN I GUESS I'VE NEVER YET SEEN ANY DEMON SO DARN...

I'M GETTING ANOTHER "BEER."

HEY, WAS THAT JUST LOVE AT FIRST SIGHT--OR SHOULD I WALK BY AGAIN...?

SO, MAYBE YOU WANNA COME CHECK OUT MY DAD'S HUMVEE? TAKE A RIDE, LET THE MAGIC...

OF COURSE IF YOU WERE A VAMPIRE I COULD RAM A WOODEN STAKE THROUGH YOUR HEART AND MAKE YOU DO THE NASTY DISINTEGRATION THING.

HEY...WHAT WAS THAT, BEAUTIFUL?

SOR-RY. LESBIAN NOW.

Art by JOHN TOTLEBEN
with DAVE STEWART

SO **WHAT** IS IT, AND WHAT DOES IT WANT?

WE'RE NOT **SURE,** BUT FROM WHAT WE'VE BEEN ABLE TO PIECE TOGETHER, THE CREATURE APPEARS TO BE--

I MEAN **HER.**

OH, YOU MEAN MISS PERSONALITY WHO MOST LIKELY HASN'T **BATHED** SINCE THE THIRTEENTH CENTURY?

...ELEVENTH CENTURY.

WHAT-EVER. BEFORE THEY HAD **SOAP.**

SHE'S...uh... SORT OF A **SLAYER.**

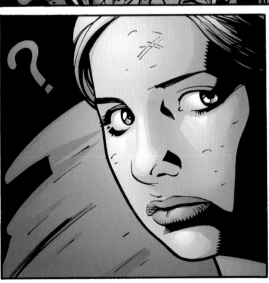

A SLAYER? **ANOTHER** SLAYER?

HOW MANY SLAYERS DO I HAVE TO DEAL WITH? *I'M* SUPPOSED TO BE THE SLAYER. FIRST YOU'RE A *CHEERLEADER*, THEN SOME GUY'S THROWING *KNIVES* AT YOU AND YOU'RE "*THE SLAYER*," BUT NO, WAIT! THERE ARE *OTHER SLAYERS*--BAD ONES, JAMAICAN ONES, *VAMPIRE* ONES, AND NOW *THIS!*

SO WHAT IS *SHE* DOING HERE, GILES? TELL ME *THAT*. DID I DIE AGAIN? IS THIS BETH'S UNWASHED TWIN? WHAT IS SHE...?

WE'RE NOT SURE.

...BASED ON HER RATHER CRUDE GOTHIC DIALECT, HER DRESS, AND...er... HER SOMEWHAT *INDELIBLE ODOR*, I'D PLACE HER SOMEWHERE IN THE ELEVENTH CENTURY. SHE HAS THE MARK OF THE SLAYER, AND CLEARLY UNDERSTANDS HOW TO FIGHT.

I'M NOT VERY UP TO SPEED ON MY PRE-ANGLICAN GOTHIC, BUT SHE'S COME A LONG WAY--EIGHT OR NINE CENTURIES AT LEAST--WHICH IMPLIES SOME SORT OF MAGIC. AND SHE'S APPARENTLY HERE TO SLAY THAT CREATURE, WHICH SHE KEEPS REFERRING TO AS "*KARFARNAUM*."

MAGAPEI!

WHAT? WHAT DOES THAT MEAN?

WELL, ah...I'M NOT ENTIRELY SURE...

GILES...?

¿Sigh¿ SHE JUST CALLED YOU A "SILLY VIRGIN"--

SHE--!?

WHERE ARE YOU GOING? *WHERE IS SHE GOING?*

UM...FAR-FAN NUUKEN?

GADJAKRAN.

WHAT DOES *THAT* MEAN?!

I DON'T KNOW, YET. THE TRUTH IS I NEVER ACTUALLY MADE IT PAST *"WEAPONS AND WEATHER"* AT THE COUNCIL'S GOTHIC COURSES...BUT I DO HAVE LOTS OF BOOKS...

UNSAR KARFARNAUM ET GUND, *NASJANDS*. NE DWALA *NASJANDS*-- SAUBS SE.

WHAT? WHAT'S...?

KA-CHUNNNGG

NNNGH!

NOW WE'RE EVEN.

WHERE IN THE PARK ARE THEY?!

WILLOW!

HOLD ON...

JUST A MOMENT...

WILLOW, WE'VE GOT TO...!!

AAEEN

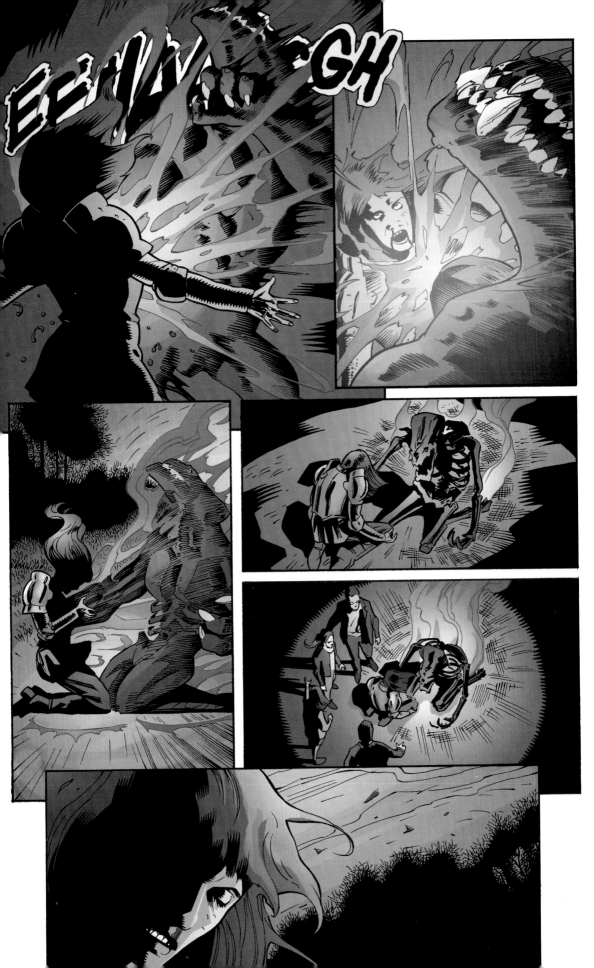

Art by RYAN SOOK and GALEN SHOWMAN
with DAVE STEWART

CEMETERY
OF
LOST LOVE

YOU OKAY, WILL?

...WHAT?

I WAS JUST TELLING YOU ABOUT MY ADVENTURE LAST NIGHT. BUT IT'S NO BIG DEAL.

SORRY, I GUESS I'M A LITTLE DISTRACTED.

MISSING OZ, HUH?

IS IT THAT OBVIOUS?

WELL, NOT *THAT* OBVIOUS... BUT YOU *DO* TALK IN YOUR SLEEP.

UGH. MONDO EMBARRASSMENT. BUT YEAH, I THINK ABOUT HIM A LOT. I REALLY MISS HIM.

I MISS HIM TOO-- BUT IN A TOTALLY DIFFERENT SORT OF WAY. MAYBE YOU SHOULD THINK ABOUT HOOKING UP WITH SOMEONE TO, YOU KNOW, CLEAR THE MIND.

OH SURE, THAT'S EASY FOR YOU TO SAY NOW THAT YOU AND RILEY ARE GIVING EACH OTHER WARM FUZZIES.

ALL WE'VE DONE IS KISS...

EWWWWWWW! LOOK! THERE'S ANOTHER ONE!

THAT'S MORE THAN ONE, WILL!

NOW I'M *REALLY* NOT HUNGRY.

EEEEEE! GET THEM OFF ME!

UMMM... I THINK THEY'RE COMING AFTER YOU, BUFFY.

WHAT THE--?

I HOPE GILES HAS AN EASY ANSWER TO THIS BIZARRE-NESS.

DON'T HORDES OF NOXIOUS BEASTS USUALLY HERALD THE END OF THE WORLD?

THE END OF THE WORLD? HERE IN SUNNYDALE? WHAT A SURPRISE.

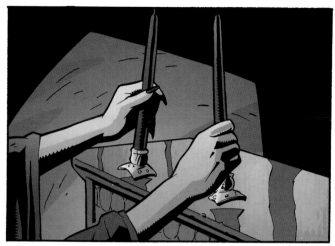

...NOW YOU KNOW AS MUCH AS WE DO.

A CONUNDRUM INDEED.

SO WHAT DO WE DO?

EVERYONE GRAB A BOOK. WE'VE GOT A LOT OF WORK TO DO.

HOW DID I KNOW YOU WERE GOING TO SAY THAT?

RUSTLE RUSTLE

GREAT, NOW THE CATS ARE GOING ALL WES CRAVEN.

OH! OH! THIS MIGHT BE IT! SOME KIND OF DEVIL...

YES... CONSIDERING THE MAGGOTS ...BEELZEBUB, THE LORD OF THE FLIES, PERHAPS?

HEY, I READ THAT!

WRONG LORD, XANDER. AND NEITHER ONE WOULD EXPLAIN THE RATS.

GOOD POINT. LET'S FILE THAT AS A POSSIBILITY AND--

I KNOW, I KNOW, KEEP LOOKING.

SCREE SCREE

RATS, RATS, RATS...

WILL YOU QUIT FOOLING AROUND? THIS IS SERIOUS!

HEY, I'M LOOKING FOR BOOKS ON RATS.

SECOND SHELF UP, THIRD BOOK FROM THE LEFT.

CEREMONIAL APPLICATIONS OF MURIDAE?

THAT'S THE ONE.

BINGO.

SHE'S COMING.

WAIT A MINUTE, WHAT ABOUT THE VODOUN!

THE WHAT?

VOODOO!

YOU MEAN LIKE ZOMBIES AND LITTLE DOLLS?

I MEAN, BUFFY'S WALKING INTO A TRAP.

KRAK

WAIT... WHAT ARE YOU HOPING TO GET OUT OF THIS?

THERE ARE THINGS THAT TONY DID TO ME THAT NO REGULAR MAN COULD DO. I MAY HAVE LOST HIM, BUT I WON'T LOSE THAT...FEELING. SO I'M TRADING YOUR SOUL FOR ETERNAL LIFE.

ETERNAL LIFE ISN'T ALL IT'S CRACKED UP TO BE.

YOU'LL NEVER KNOW.

HOW--?

I'M STRONGER THAN I LOOK.

YOUR TURN.

CAN'T FIGHT YOUR OWN BATTLES, HUH--?

AW, NOW THAT'S GROSS.

YOU'VE RUINED EVERY-THING.

OW!

HEY, SPIKE, ARE YOU OKAY?

GET YOUR MITTS OFF ME.

I WAS JUST TRYING TO BE NICE.

I DON'T NEED YOUR CHARITY. I'VE BEEN DOING QUITE WELL FOR CENTURIES WITHOUT IT.

YEAH, WELL, THANKS FOR HELPING OUT.

HA! DON'T FLATTER YOURSELF, BLONDIE. I JUST CAME TO FIGHT ZOMBIES.

WHATEVER MAKES YOU FEEL BETTER, SPIKE.

Stake out these Buffy the Vampire Slayer and Angel trade paperbacks

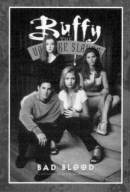

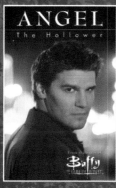

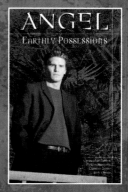

ALIENS
LABYRINTH
Woodring • Plunkett
136-page color paperback
ISBN: 1-85286-844-9
NIGHTMARE ASYLUM
(formerly Aliens: Book Two)
Verheiden • Beauvais
112-page color paperback
ISBN: 1-85286-765-5
OUTBREAK
(formerly Aliens: Book One)
Verheiden • Nelson
168-page color paperback
ISBN: 1-85286-756-6
ALIENS VS PREDATOR
ALIENS VS PREDATOR
Stradley • Norwood • Warner
176-page color paperback
ISBN: 1-85286-413-3
*THE DEADLIEST
OF THE SPECIES*
Claremont • Guice • Barreto
320-page color paperback
ISBN: 1-85286-953-4
WAR
Various
200-page color paperback
ISBN: 1-85286-703-5
ETERNAL
Edginton • Maleev
88-page color paperback
ISBN: 1-84023-111-4
*ALIENS VS. PREDATOR
VS. TERMINTAOR*
Schultz • Ruby • Ivy
96-page color paperback
ISBN: 1-84023-313-3
ANGEL
THE HOLLOWER
Golden • Gomez • Florea
88-page color paperback
ISBN: 1-84023-163-7
SURROGATES
Golden •Zanier •
Owens • Gomez
80-page color paperback
ISBN: 1-84023-234-X
**BUFFY THE VAMPIRE SLAY-
ER**
THE DUST WALTZ
Brereton • Gomez
80-page color paperback
ISBN: 1-84023-057-6
THE REMAINING SUNLIGHT
Watson • Van Meter •
Bennett • Ross
88-page color paperback
ISBN: 1-84023-078-9
THE ORIGIN
Golden • Brereton •
Bennett • Ketcham
80-page color paperback
ISBN: 1-84023-105-X
RING OF FIRE
Petrie • Sook
80-page color paperback
ISBN: 1-84023-200-5
UNINVITED GUESTS
Watson • Brereton •
Gomez • Florea
96-page color paperback

ISBN: 1-84023-140-8
BAD BLOOD
Watson • Bennett • Ketcham
88-page color paperback
ISBN: 1-84023-179-3
CRASH TEST DEMONS
Watson • Richards • Pimentel
88-page color paperback
ISBN: 1-84023-199-8
PALE REFLECTIONS
Watson • Richards • Pimentel
96-page color paperback
ISBN: 1-84023-236-6
THE BLOOD OF CARTHAGE
Golden • Richards • Pimentel
128-page color paperback
ISBN: 1-84023-281-1
STAR WARS
*BOBA FETT: ENEMY OF
THE EMPIRE*
Wagner • Gibson • Nadeau
112-page color paperback
ISBN: 1-84023-125-4
BOUNTY HUNTERS
Stradley • Truman • Schultz •
Mangels •Nadeau • Rubi • Saltares
112-page color paperback
ISBN: 1-84023-238-2
CHEWBACCA
Macan • Various
96-page color paperback
ISBN: 1-84023-274-9
CRIMSON EMPIRE
Richardson • Stradley •
Gulacy • Russell
160-page color paperback
ISBN: 1-84023-006-1
CRIMSON EMPIRE II
Richardson • Stradley •
Gulacy • Emberlin
160-page color paperback
ISBN: 1-84023-126-2
DARK EMPIRE
Veitch • Kennedy
184-page color paperback
ISBN: 1-84023-098-3
DARK EMPIRE II
Veitch • Kennedy
168-page color paperback
ISBN: 1-84023-099-1
*EPISODE I
THE PHANTOM MENACE*
Gilroy • Damaggio • Williamson
112-page color paperback
ISBN: 1-84023-025-8
EPISODE I ADVENTURES
152-page color paperback
ISBN: 1-84023-177-7
JEDI ACADEMY – LEVIATHAN
Anderson • Carrasco • Heike
96-page color paperback
ISBN: 1-84023-138-6
THE LAST COMMAND
Baron • Biukovic • Shanower
144-page color paperback
ISBN: 1-84023-007-X
*MARA JADE:
BY THE EMPEROR'S HAND*
Zahn • Stackpole • Ezquerra
144-page color paperback
ISBN: 1-84023-011-8

PRELUDE TO REBELLION
Strnad • Winn • Jones
144-page color paperback
ISBN: 1-84023-139-4
SHADOWS OF THE EMPIRE
Wagner • Plunkett • Russell
160-page color paperback
ISBN: 1-84023-009-6
*SHADOWS OF THE EMPIRE:
EVOLUTION*
Perry • Randall • Simmons
120-page color paperback
ISBN: 1-84023-135-1
*TALES OF THE JEDI:
DARK LORDS OF THE SITH*
Veitch • Anderson • Gossett
160-page color paperback
ISBN: 1-84023-129-7
*TALES OF THE JEDI:
FALL OF THE SITH*
Anderson • Heike • Carrasco, Jr.
136-page color paperback
ISBN: 1-84023-012-6
*TALES OF THE JEDI: THE
GOLDEN AGE OF THE SITH*
Anderson • Gossett •
Carrasco • Heike
144-page color paperback
ISBN: 1-84023-000-2
*TALES OF THE JEDI:
THE SITH WAR*
152-page color paperback
ISBN: 1-84023-130-0
UNION
Stackpole • Teranishi • Chuckry
96-page color paperback
ISBN: 1-84023-233-1
VADER'S QUEST
Macan • Gibbons • McKie
96-page color paperback
ISBN: 1-84023-149-1
*X-WING ROGUE SQUADRON:
THE WARRIOR PRINCESS*
Stackpole • Tolson •
Nadeau • Ensign
96-page color paperback
ISBN: 1-85286-997-6
*X-WING ROGUE SQUADRON:
REQUIEM FOR A ROGUE*
Stackpole • Strnad • Erskine
112-page color paperback
ISBN: 1-84023-026-6
*X-WING ROGUE SQUADRON:
IN THE EMPIRE'S SERVICE*
Stackpole • Nadeau • Ensign
96-page color paperback
ISBN: 1-84023-008-8
*X-WING ROGUE SQUADRON:
BLOOD AND HONOR*
Stackpole • Crespo •
Hall • Johnson
96-page color paperback
ISBN: 1-84023-010-X
*X-WING ROGUE SQUADRON:
MASQUERADE*
Stackpole •Johnson • Martin
96-page color paperback
ISBN: 1-84023-201-3
*X-WING ROGUE SQUADRON:
MANDATORY RETIREMENT*
Stackpole • Crespo • Nadeau
96-page color paperback
ISBN: 1-84023-239-0

All publications are available through most good bookshops or
direct from our mail-order service at Titan Books. For a free
graphic-novels catalogue or to order, telephone 01536 764 646
with your credit-card details or contact Titan Books Mail Order,
Unit 6 Pipewell Industrial Estate, Desborough, Kettering,
Northants, NN14 2SW, quoting reference BA/GN.